LIBRARY OF DOOM

GRAPHIC NOVELS

THE OLDEST TRICK

TEXT BY
STEVE BREZENOFF

ART BY
PATRICIO CLAREY

raintree
a Capstone company — publishers for children

Raintree is an imprint of Capstone Global Library Limited,
a company incorporated in England and Wales having its
registered office at 264 Banbury Road, Oxford, OX2 7DY –
Registered company number: 6695582

www.raintree.co.uk
myorders@raintree.co.uk

Edited by Abby Huff
Designed by Hilary Wacholz
Original illustrations © Capstone Global Library Limited 2023
Originated by Capstone Global Library Ltd

978 1 3982 4773 4 (hardback)
978 1 3982 4774 1 (paperback)

British Library Cataloguing in Publication Data
A full catalogue record for this book is available from the
British Library.

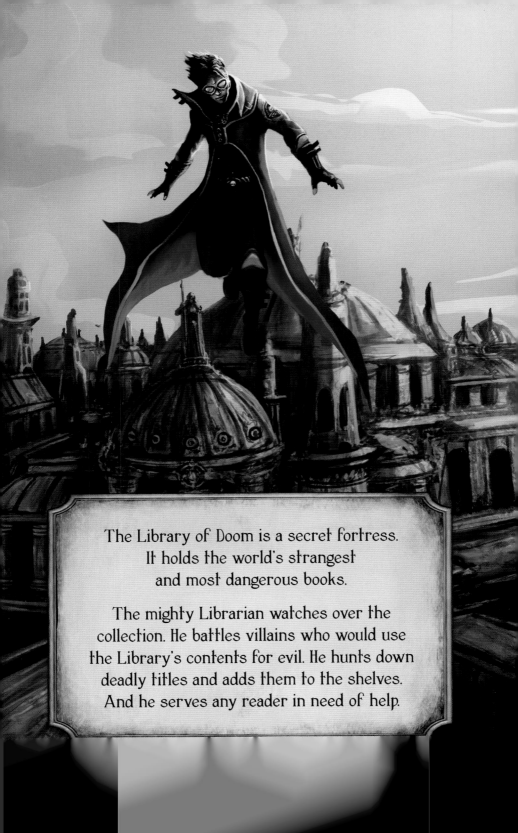

The Library of Doom is a secret fortress.
It holds the world's strangest
and most dangerous books.

The mighty Librarian watches over the
collection. He battles villains who would use
the Library's contents for evil. He hunts down
deadly titles and adds them to the shelves.
And he serves any reader in need of help.

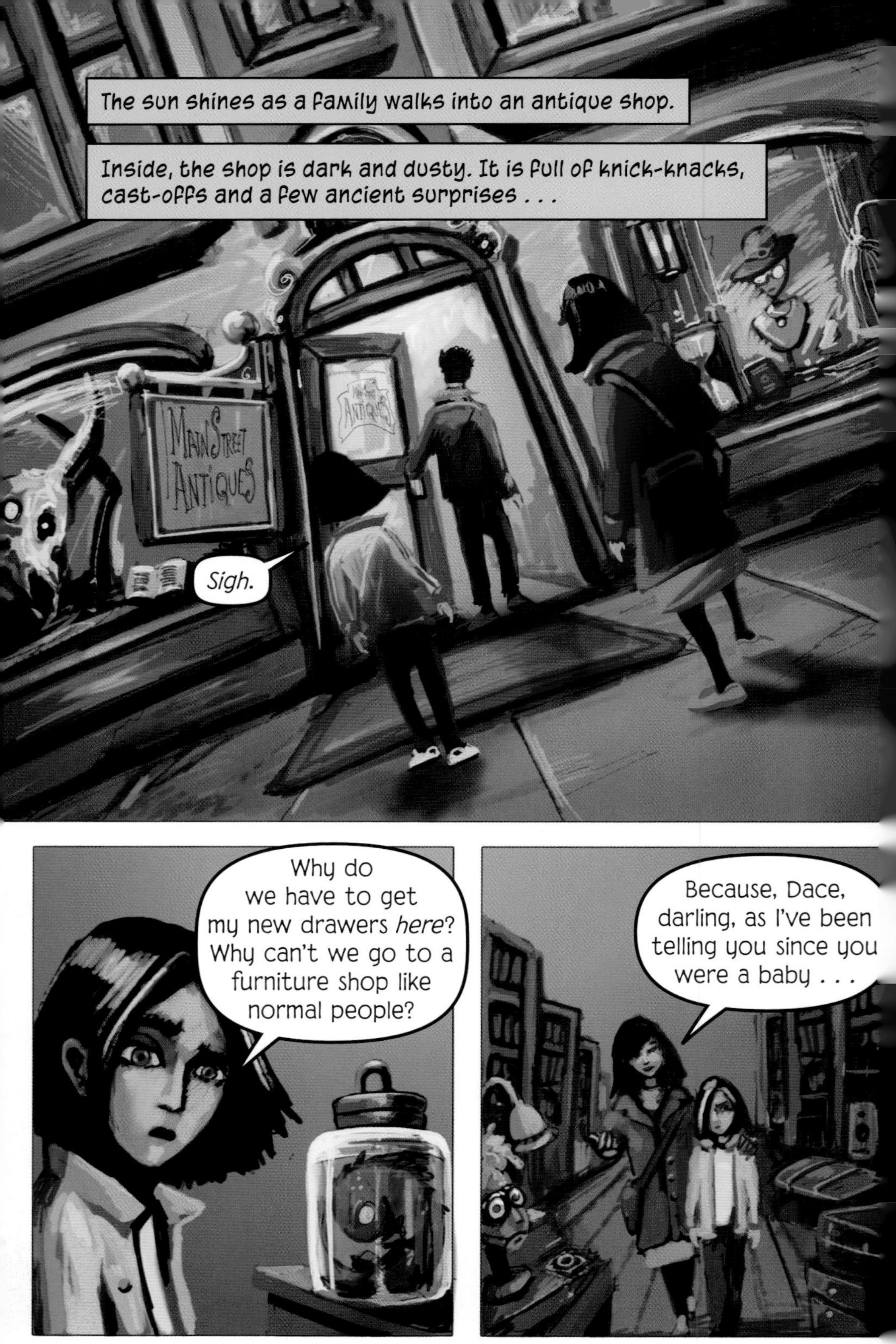

The sun shines as a family walks into an antique shop.
Inside, the shop is dark and dusty. It is full of knick-knacks, cast-offs and a few ancient surprises . . .
Main Street Antiques
Sigh.
Why do we have to get my new drawers *here*? Why can't we go to a furniture shop like normal people?
Because, Dace, darling, as I've been telling you since you were a baby . . .

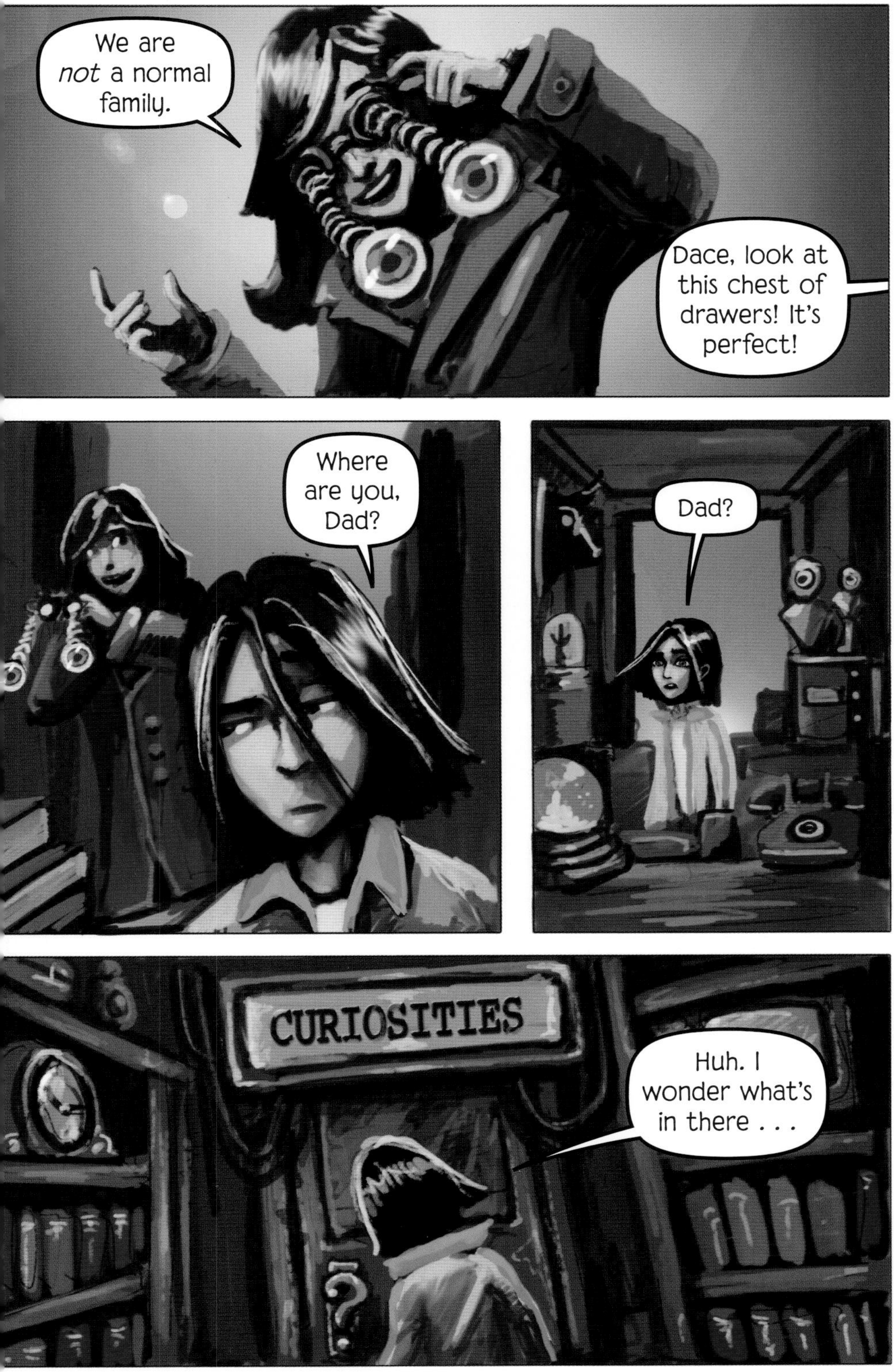
We are *not* a normal family.
Dace, look at this chest of drawers! It's perfect!
Where are you, Dad?
Dad?
CURIOSITIES
Huh. I wonder what's in there . . .

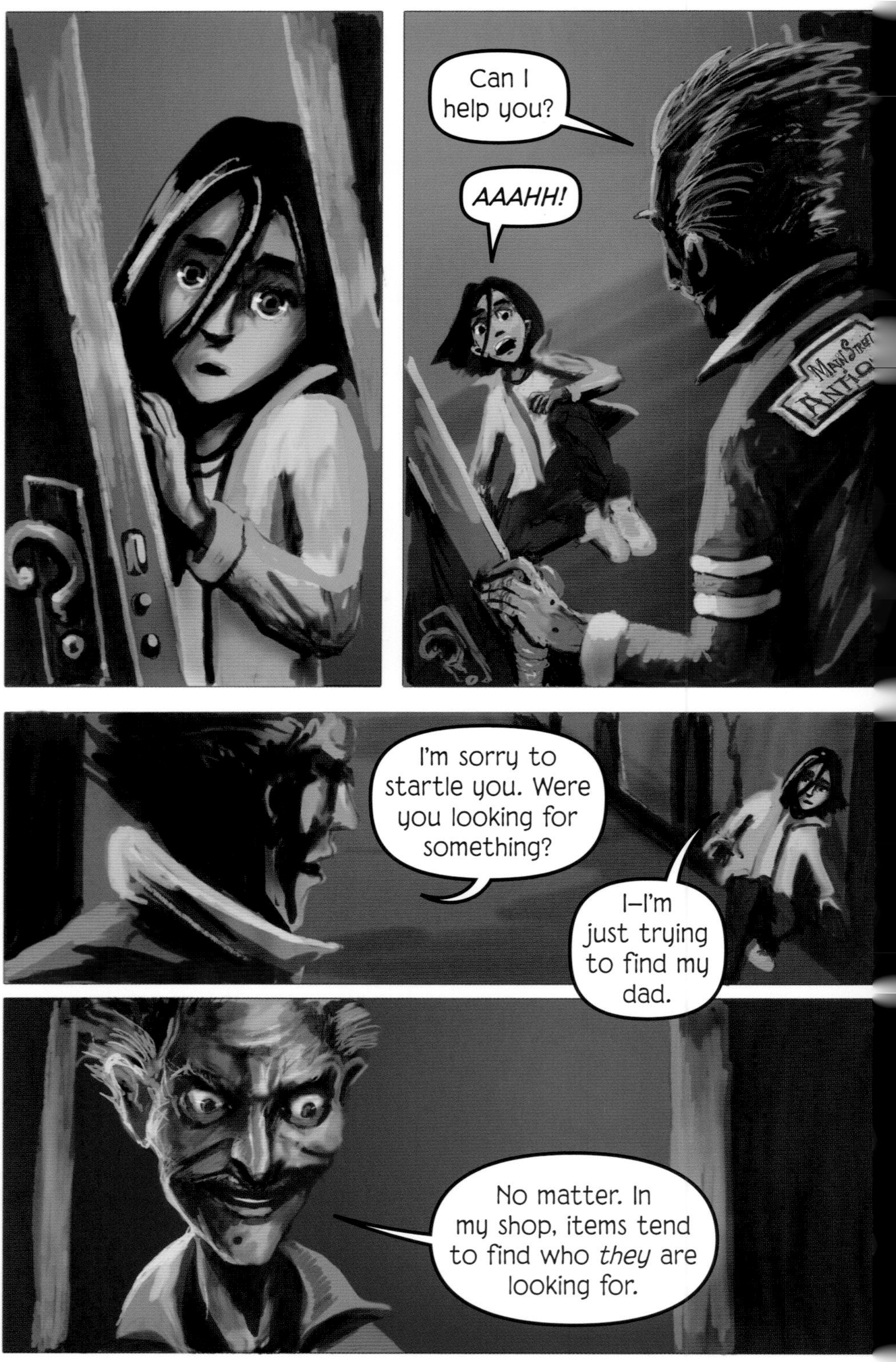
Can I help you?
AAAHH!
I'm sorry to startle you. Were you looking for something?
I–I'm just trying to find my dad.
No matter. In my shop, items tend to find who *they* are looking for.

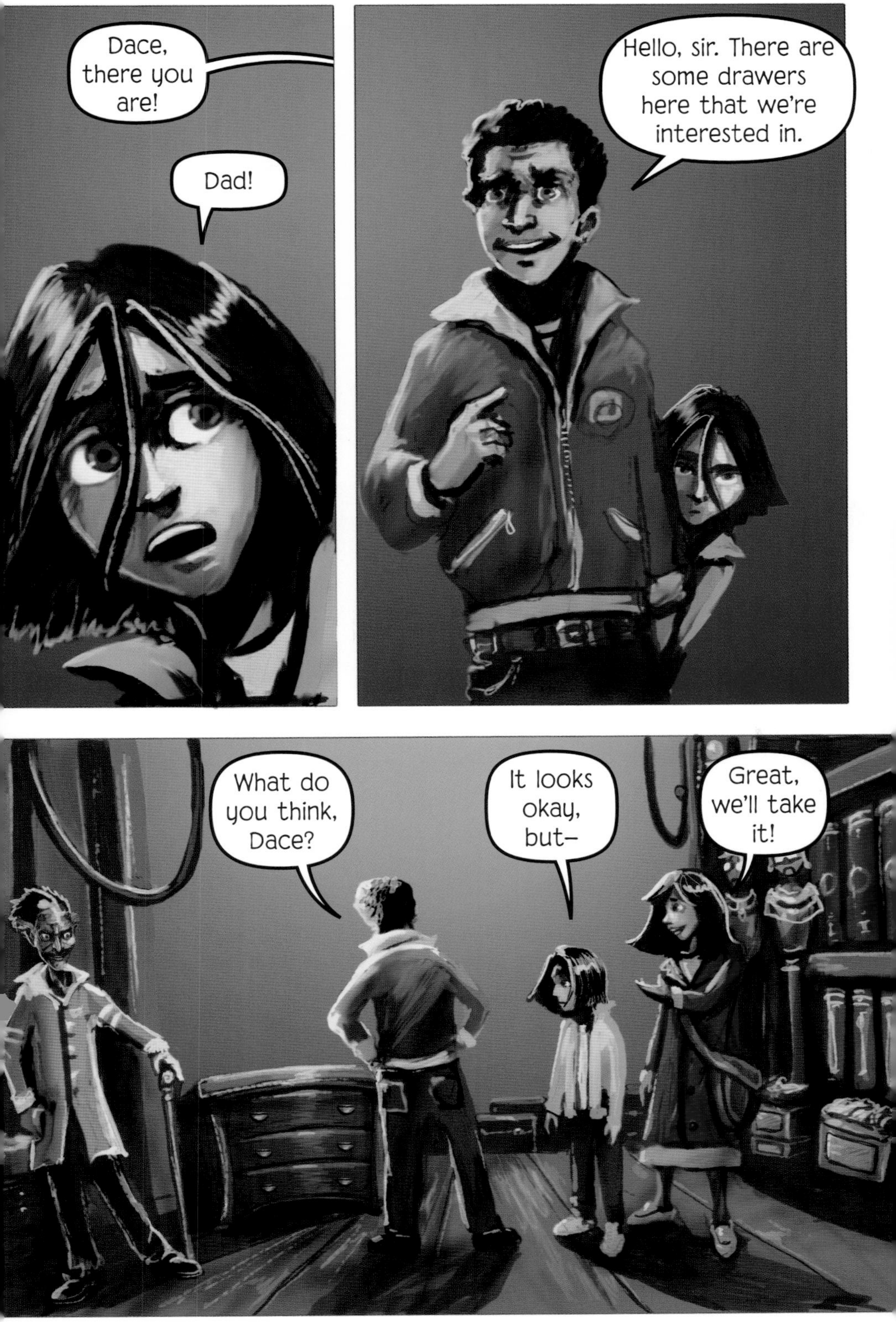
Dace, there you are!
Dad!
Hello, sir. There are some drawers here that we're interested in.
What do you think, Dace?
It looks okay, but–
Great, we'll take it!

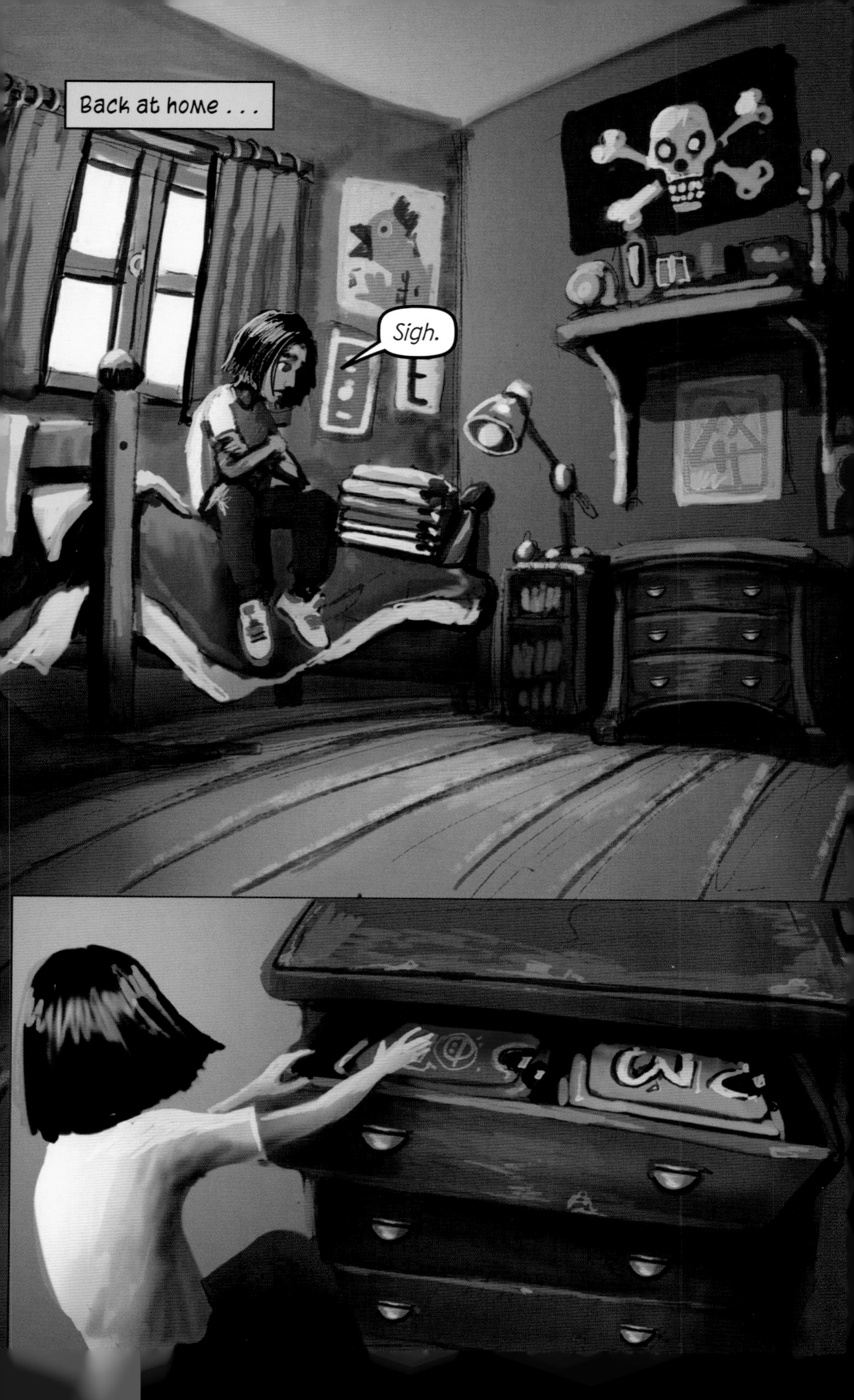

Back at home . . .
Sigh.

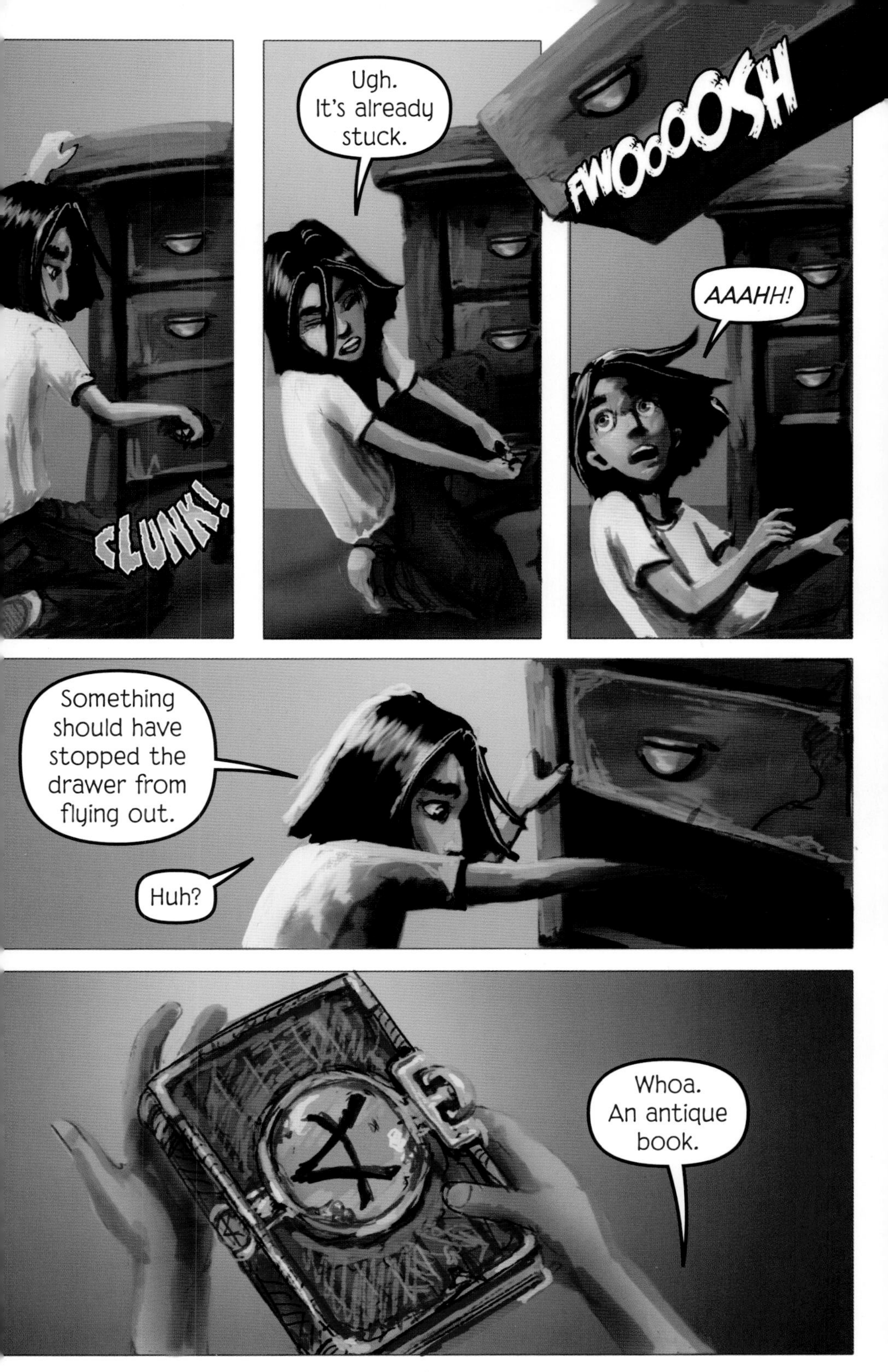
CLUNK!
Ugh. It's already stuck.
FWOoOOSH
AAAHH!
Something should have stopped the drawer from flying out.
Huh?
Whoa. An antique book.

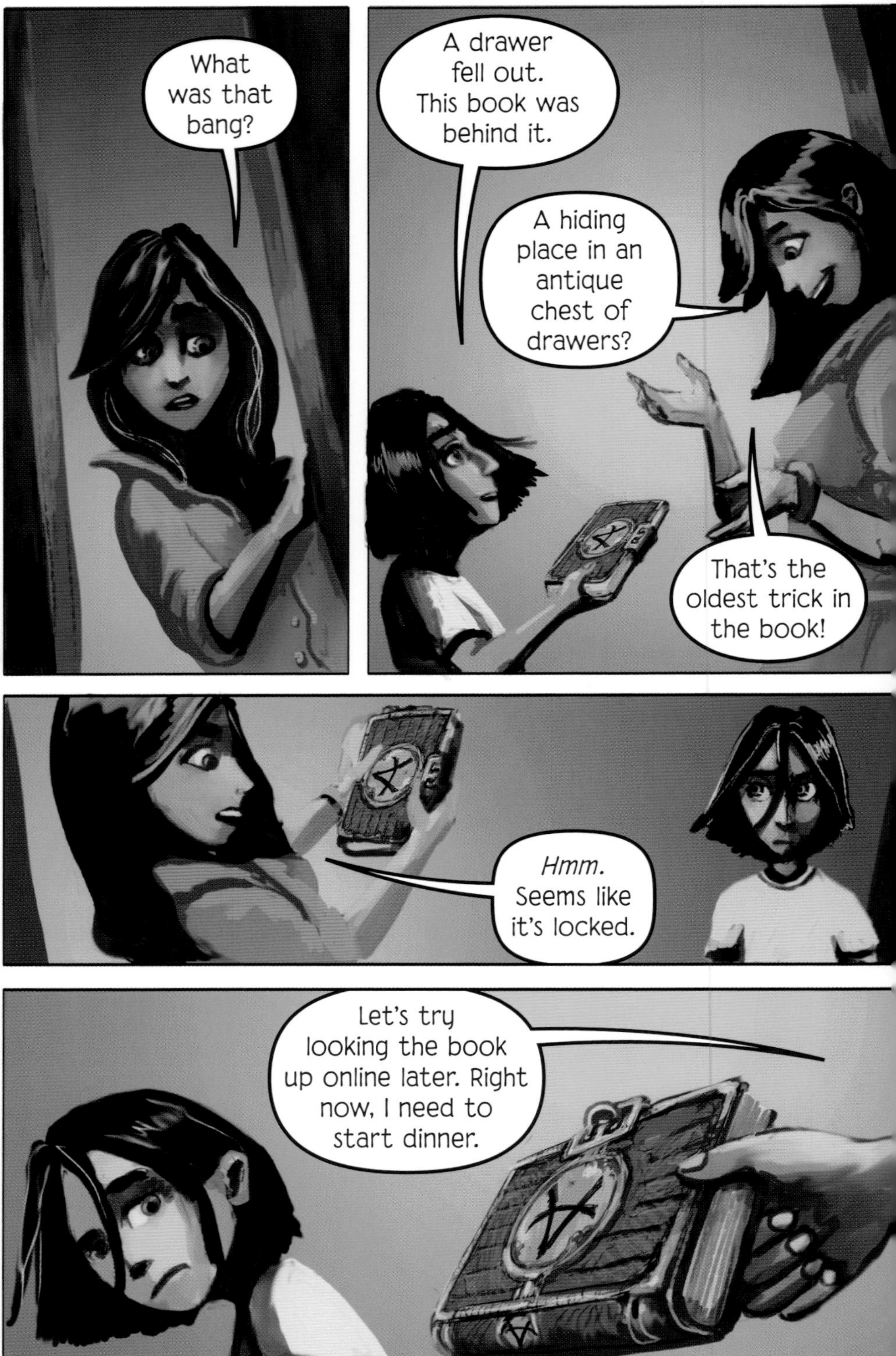
What was that bang?
A drawer fell out. This book was behind it.
A hiding place in an antique chest of drawers?
That's the oldest trick in the book!
Hmm. Seems like it's locked.
Let's try looking the book up online later. Right now, I need to start dinner.

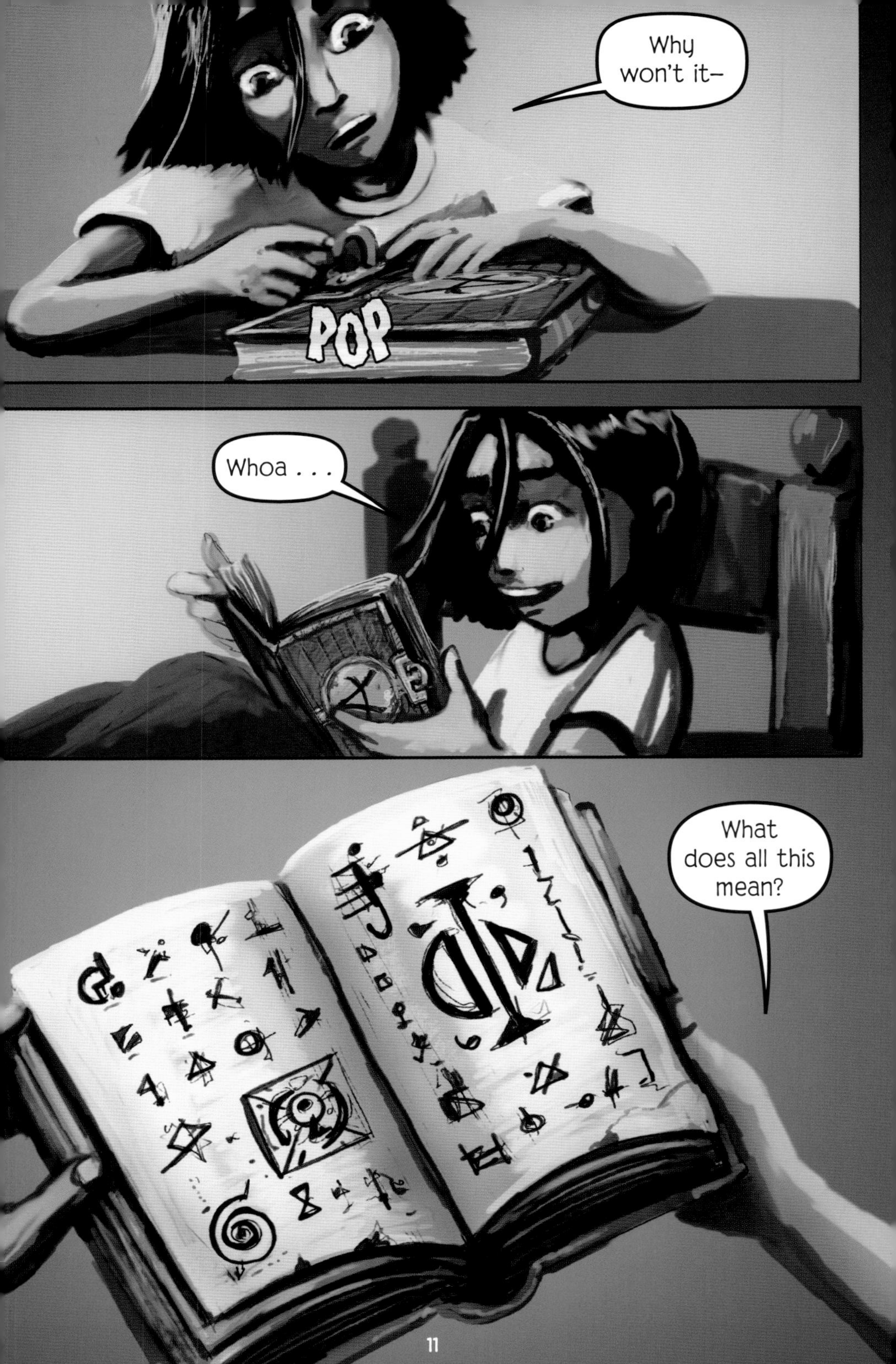
Why won't it–
POP
Whoa . . .
What does all this mean?

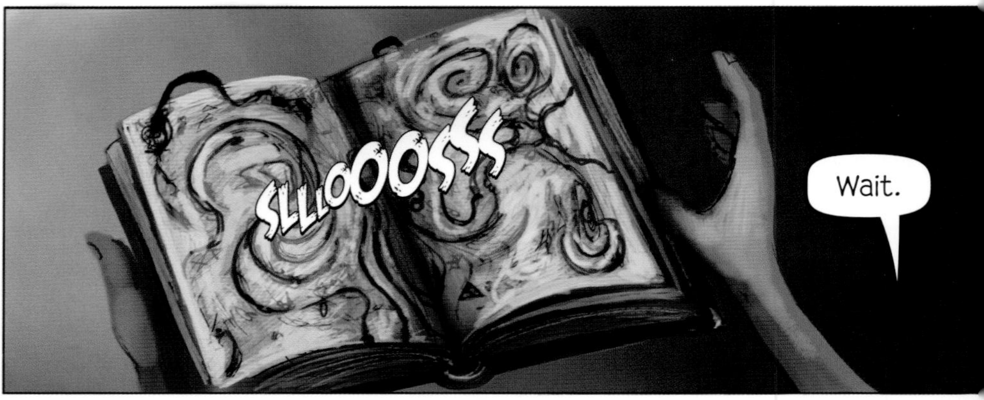
SLLLOOOSSS
Wait.

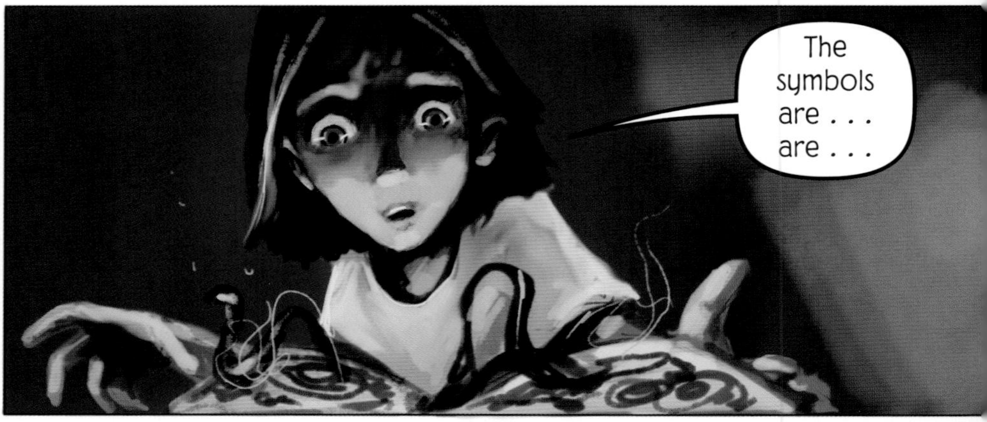
The symbols are . . . are . . .

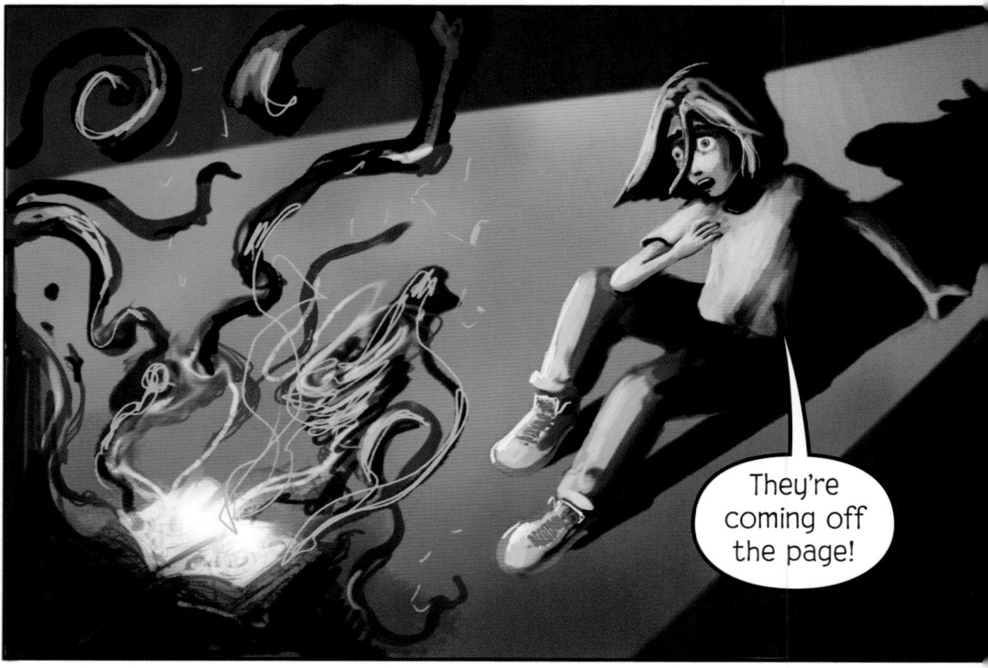
They're coming off the page!

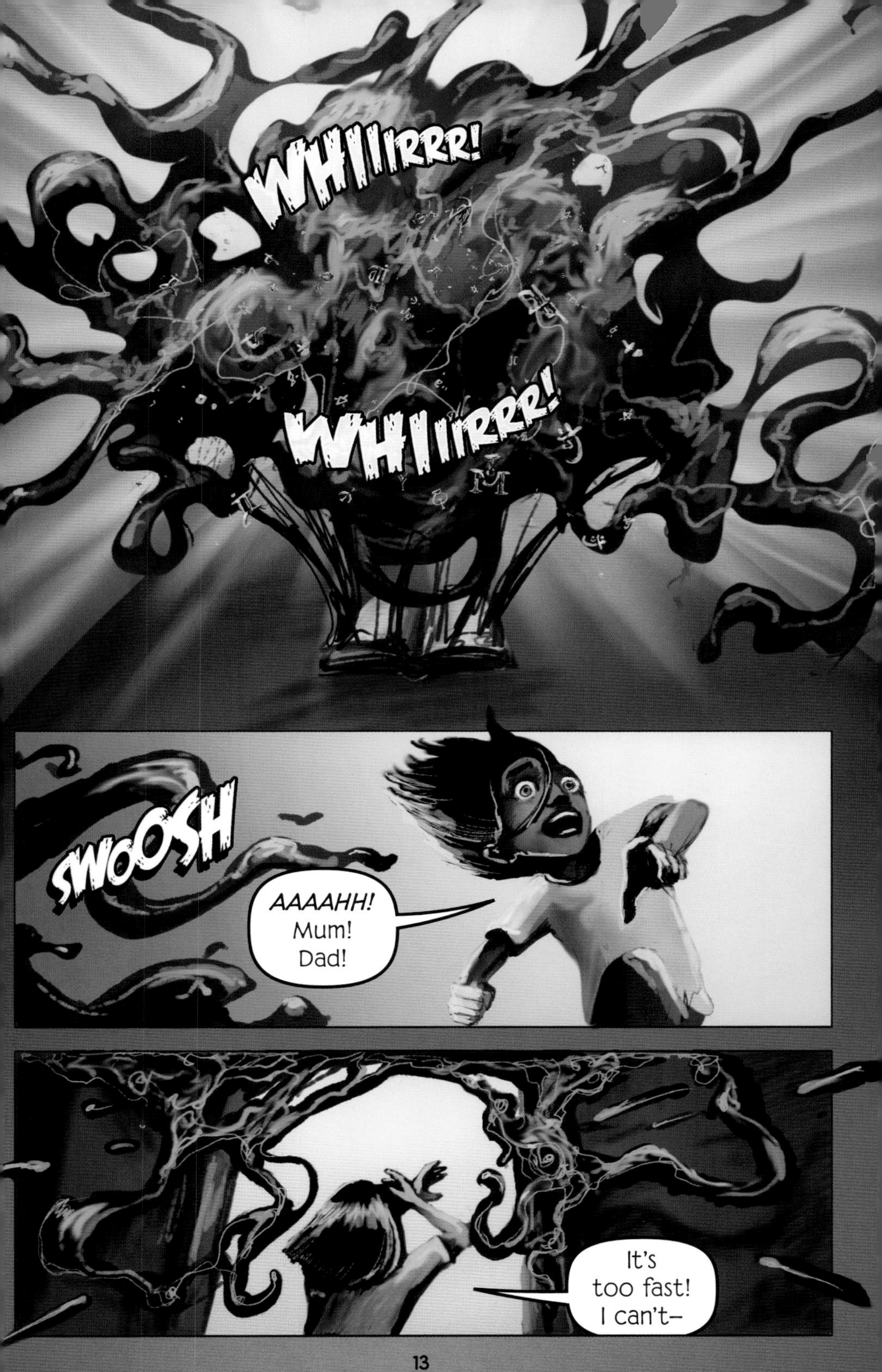
WHIIIRRR!
WHIIIRRR!
SWOOSH
AAAAHH! Mum! Dad!
It's too fast! I can't–

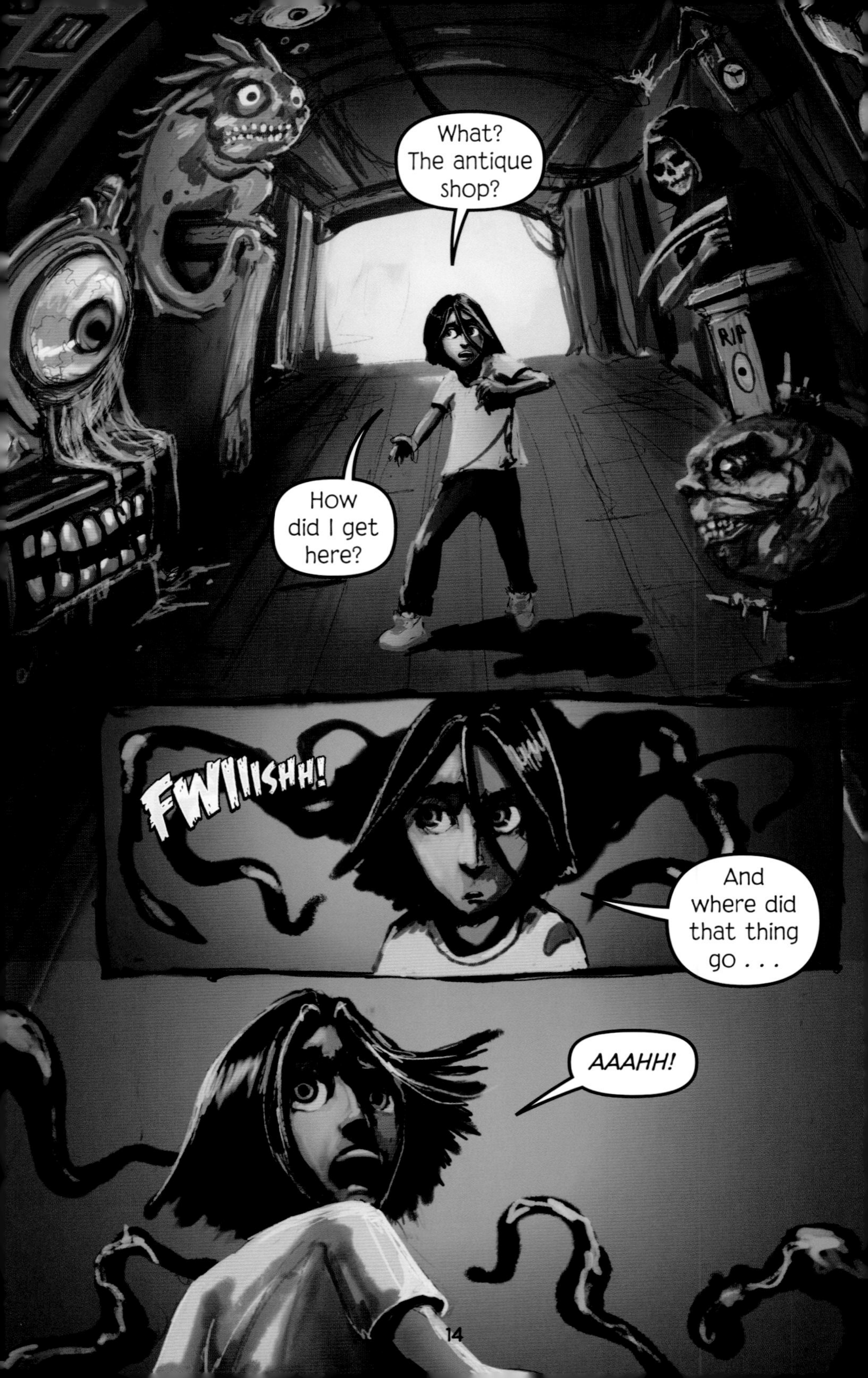

What? The antique shop?
How did I get here?
FWIIISHH!
And where did that thing go . . .
AAAHH!

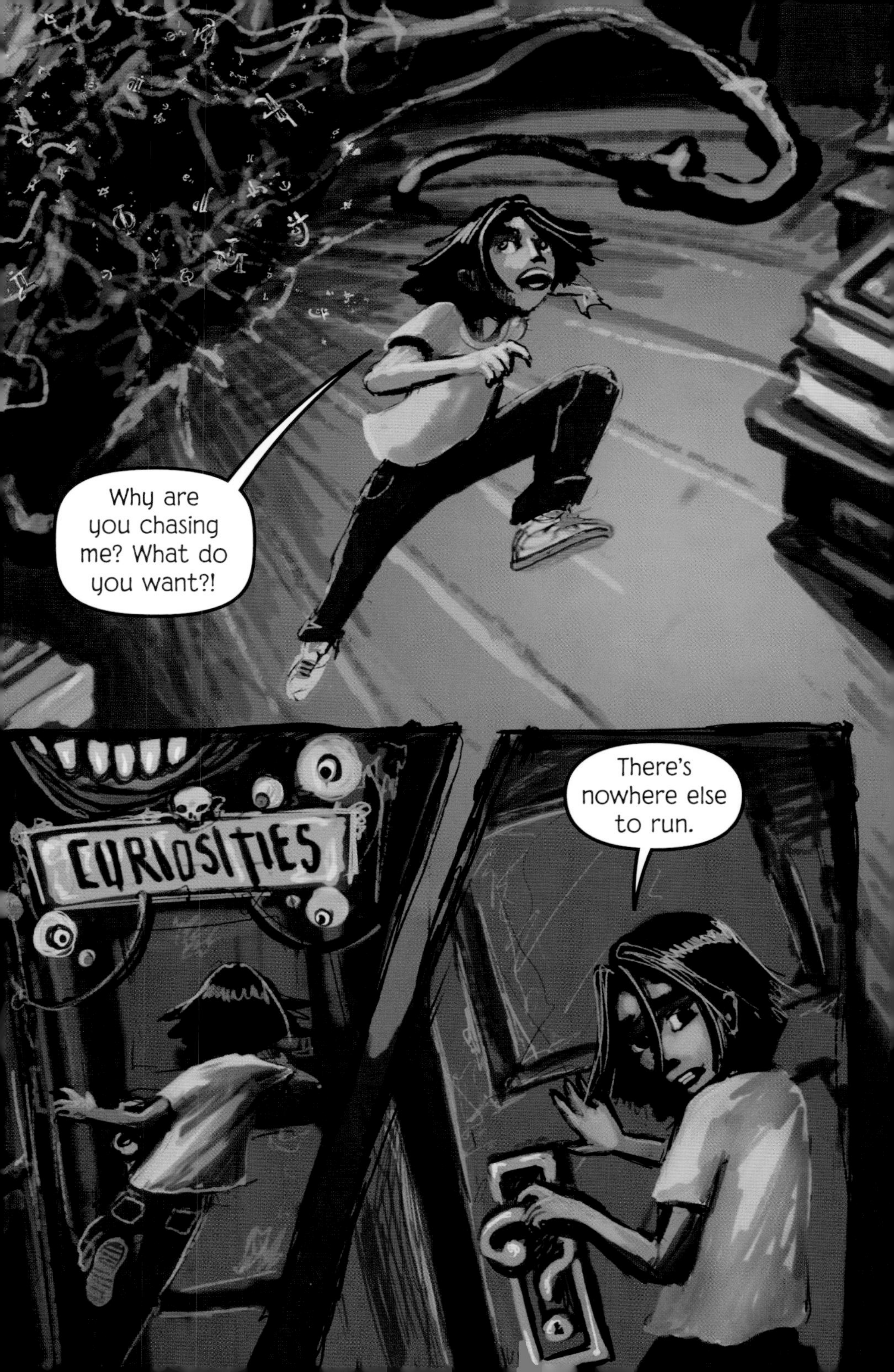
Why are you chasing me? What do you want?!
CURIOSITIES
There's nowhere else to run.

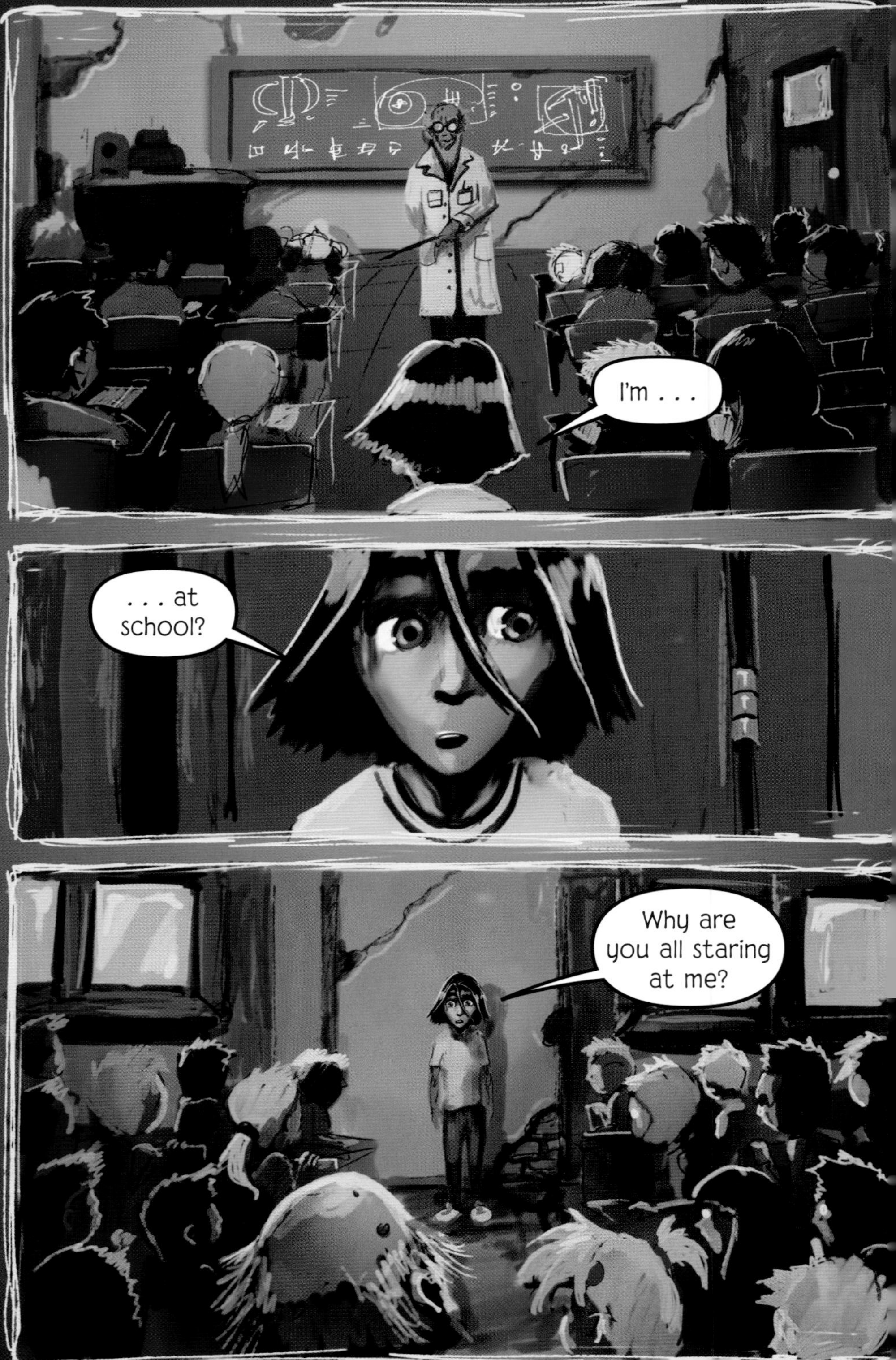
I'm . . .
. . . at school?
Why are you all staring at me?

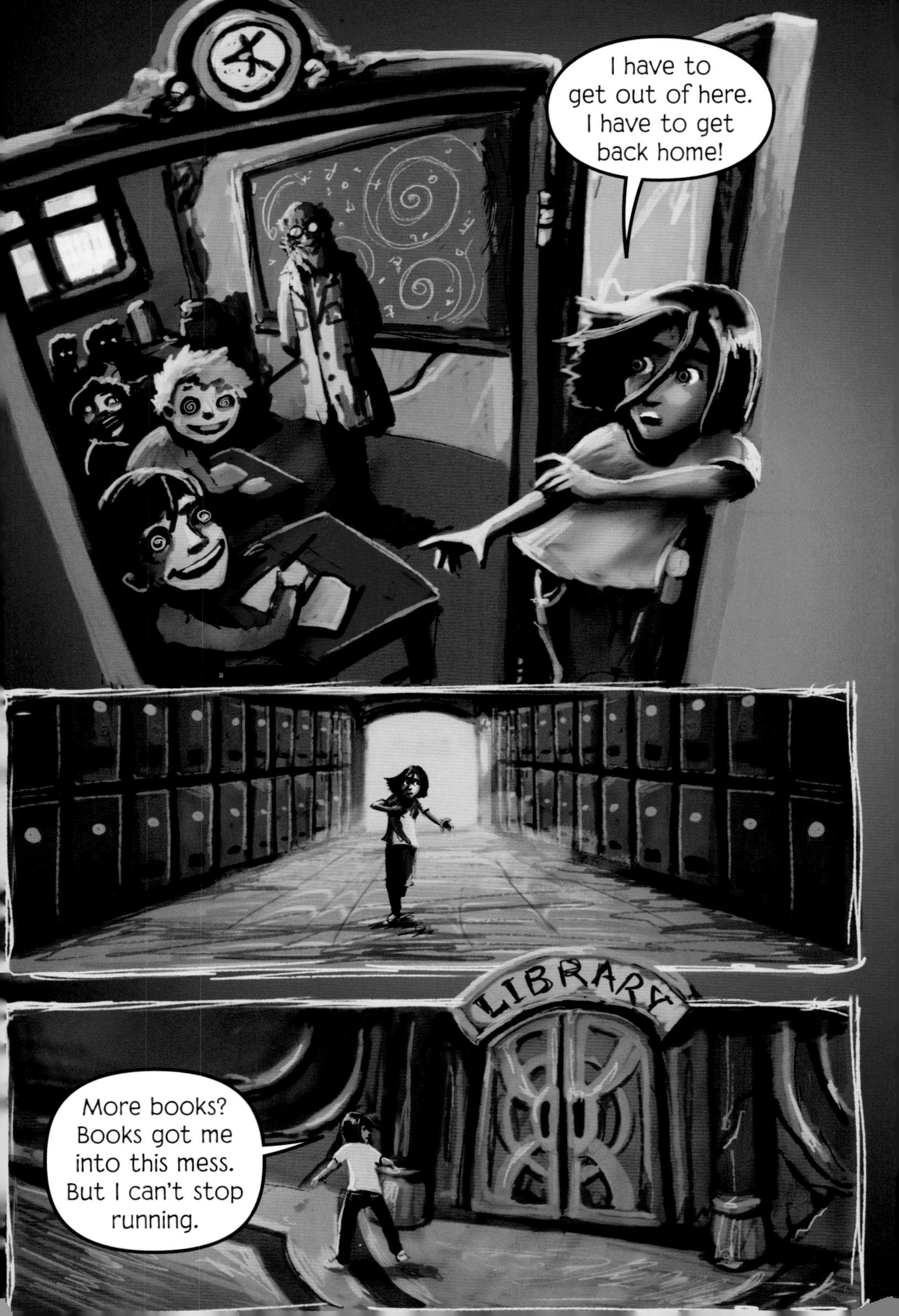

I have to get out of here. I have to get back home!
LIBRARY
More books? Books got me into this mess. But I can't stop running.

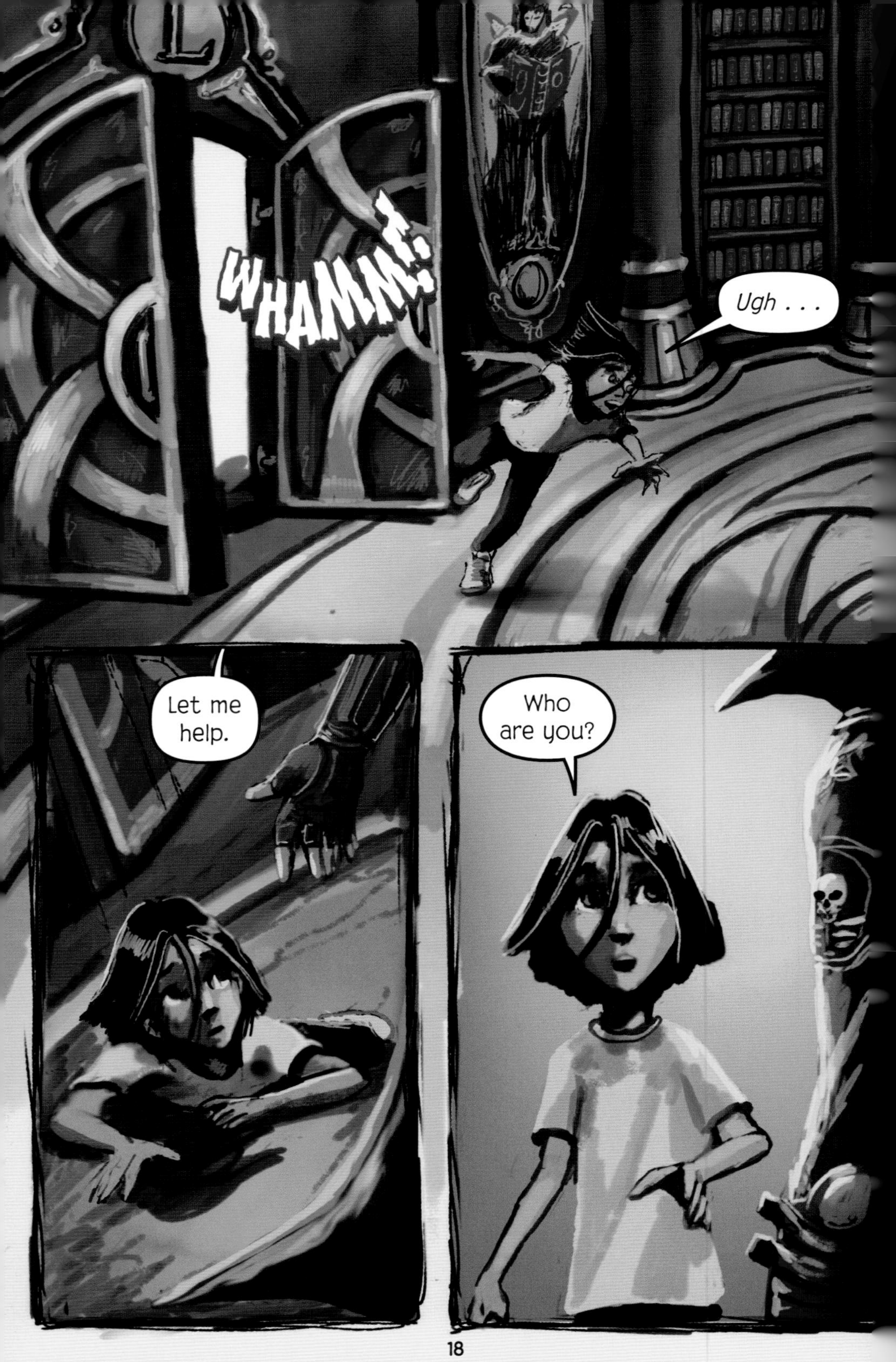
WHAMM!
Ugh . . .
Let me help.
Who are you?

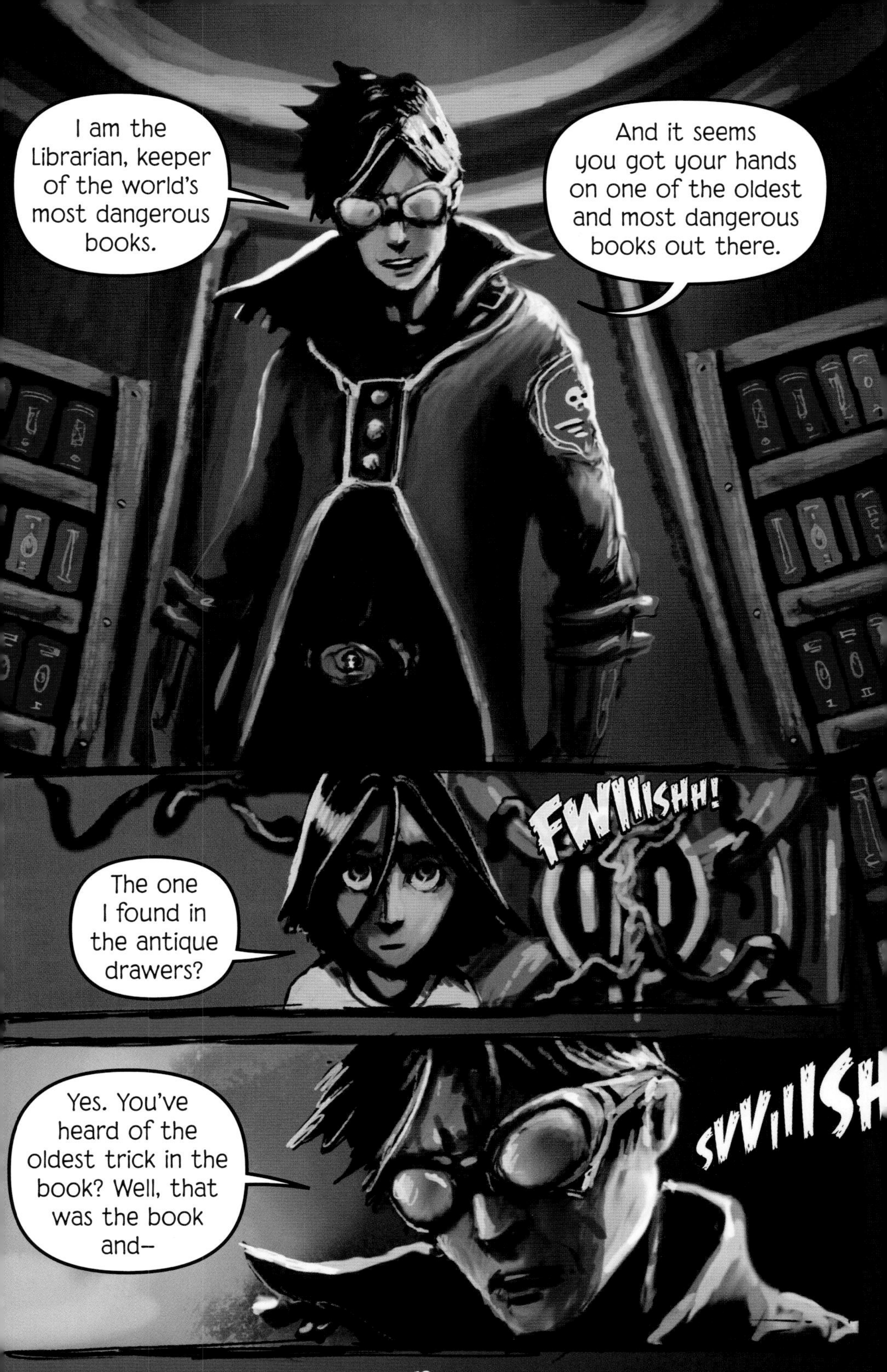
I am the Librarian, keeper of the world's most dangerous books.
And it seems you got your hands on one of the oldest and most dangerous books out there.
The one I found in the antique drawers?
FWIIISHH!
Yes. You've heard of the oldest trick in the book? Well, that was the book and–
SVVIIISH

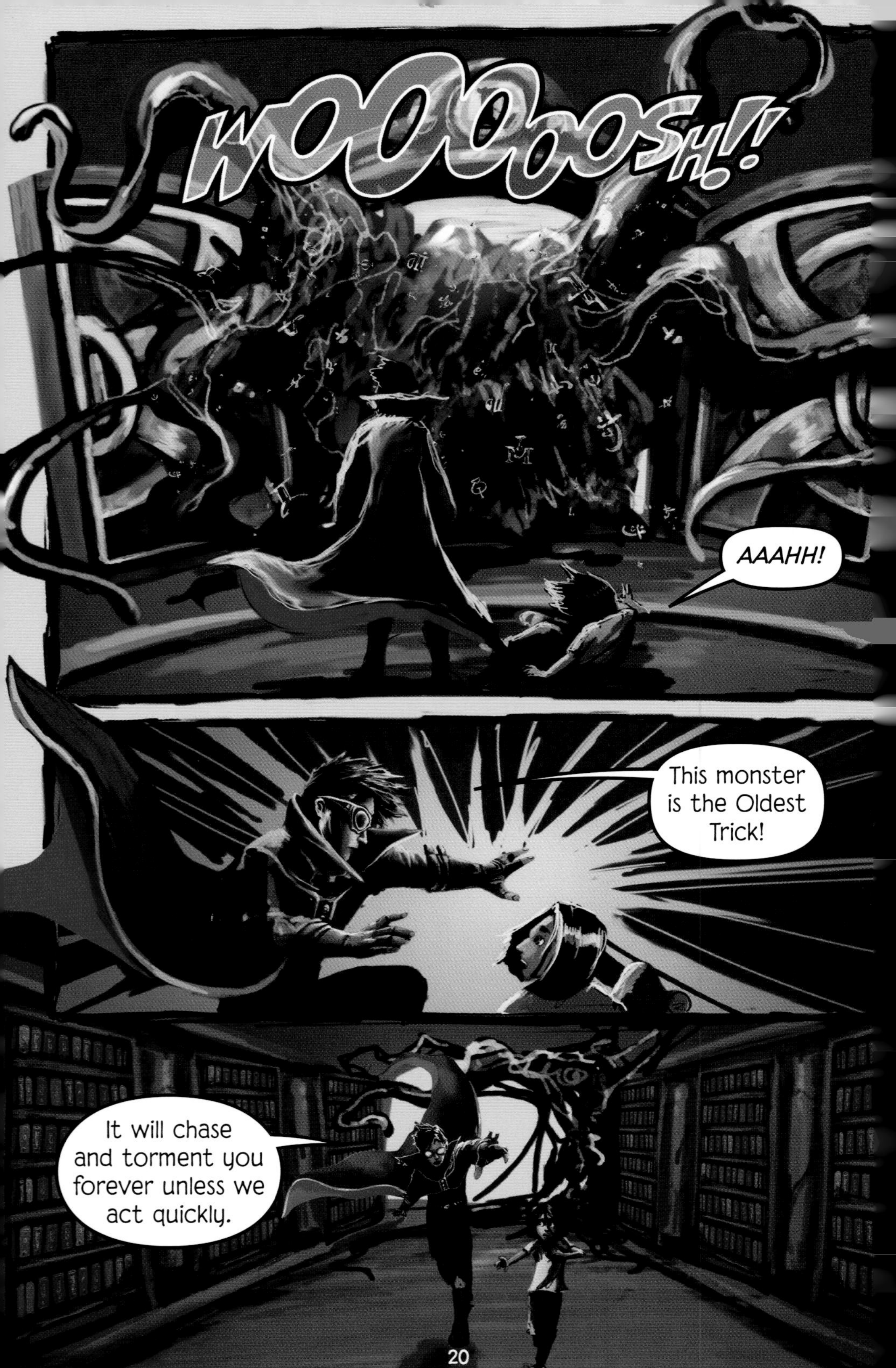
WOOOOOOSH!!
AAAHH!
This monster is the Oldest Trick!
It will chase and torment you forever unless we act quickly.

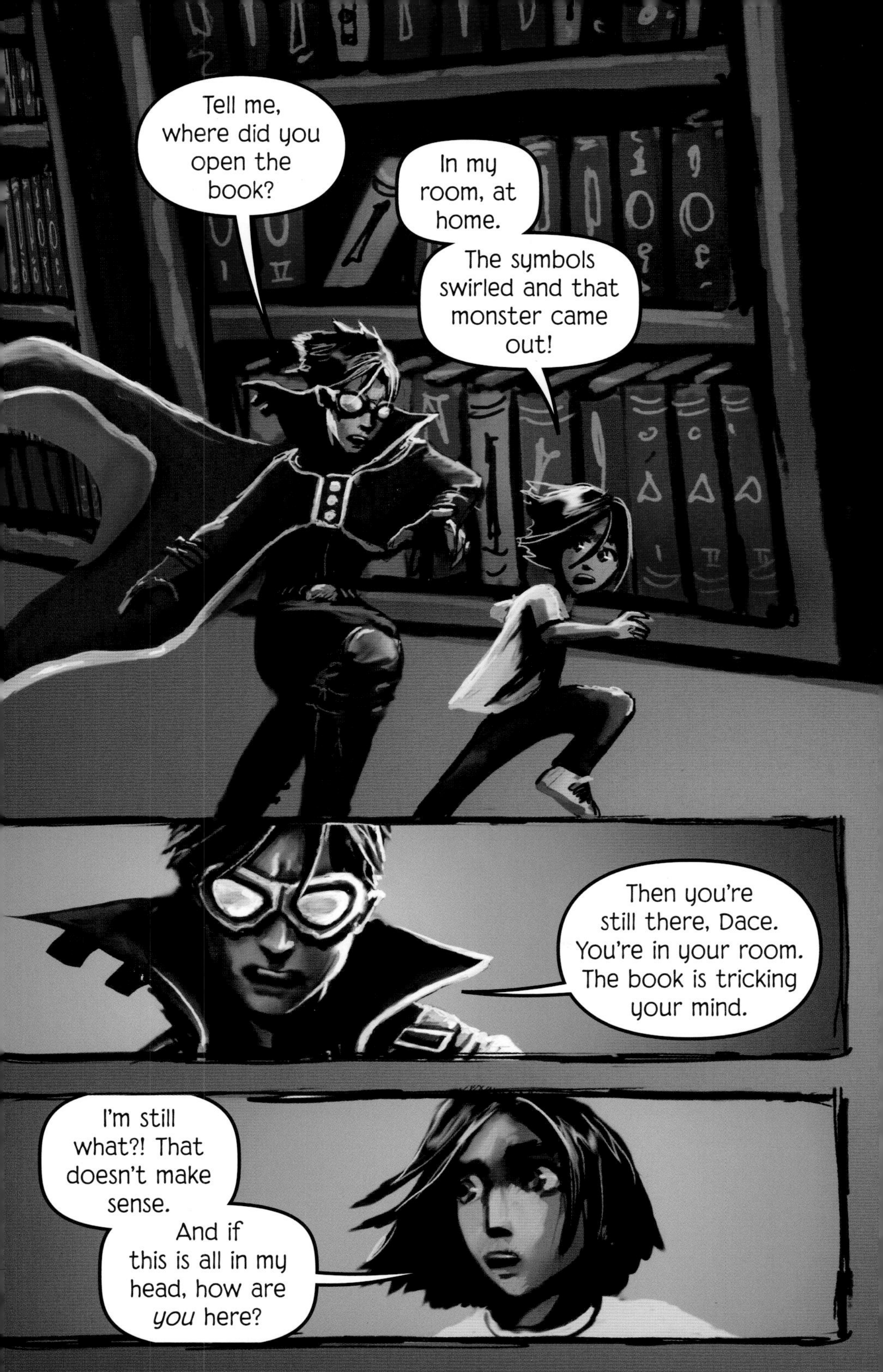
Tell me, where did you open the book?
In my room, at home.
The symbols swirled and that monster came out!
Then you're still there, Dace. You're in your room. The book is tricking your mind.
I'm still what?! That doesn't make sense.
And if this is all in my head, how are *you* here?

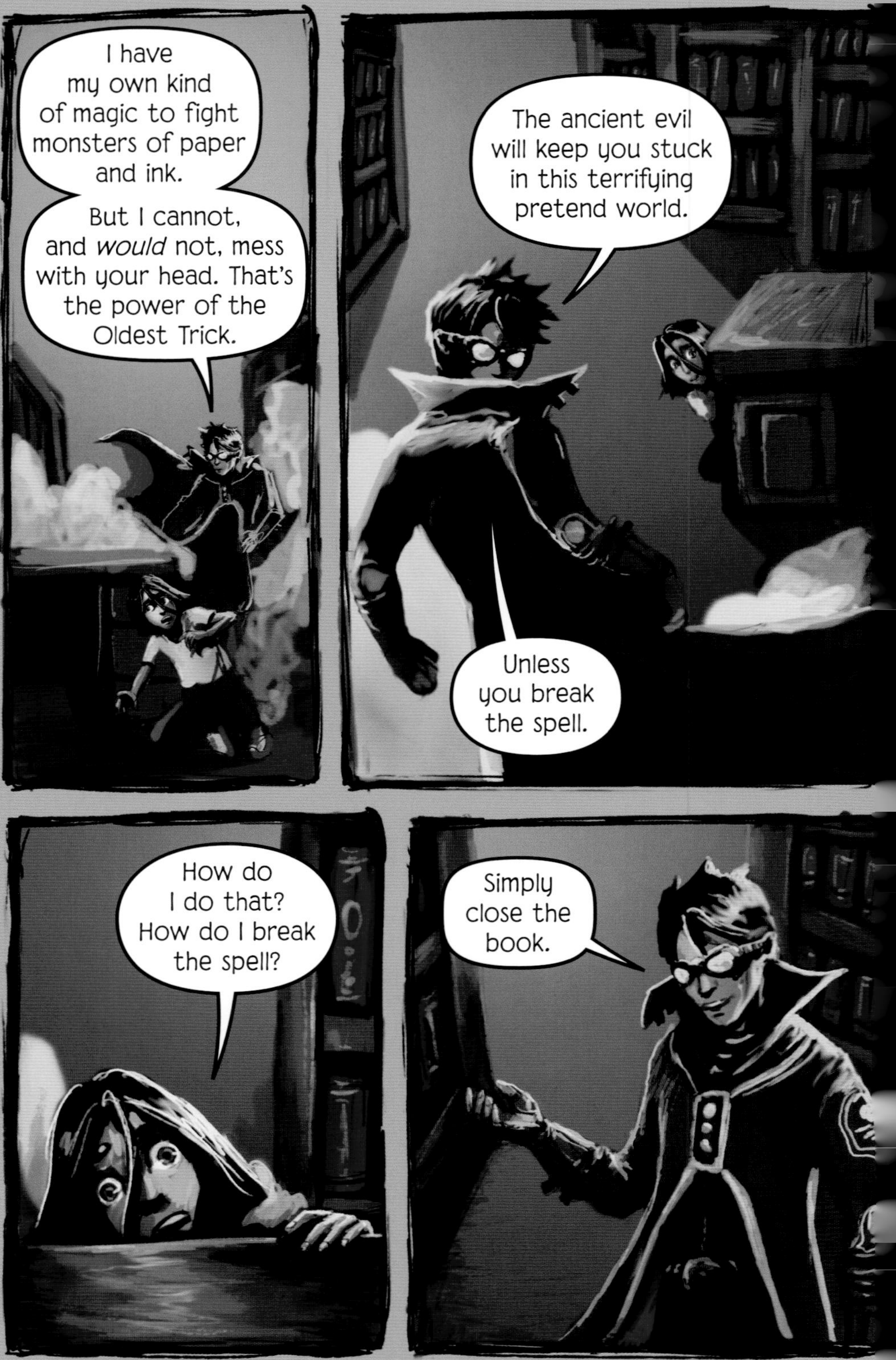
I have my own kind of magic to fight monsters of paper and ink.
But I cannot, and *would* not, mess with your head. That's the power of the Oldest Trick.
The ancient evil will keep you stuck in this terrifying pretend world.
Unless you break the spell.
How do I do that? How do I break the spell?
Simply close the book.

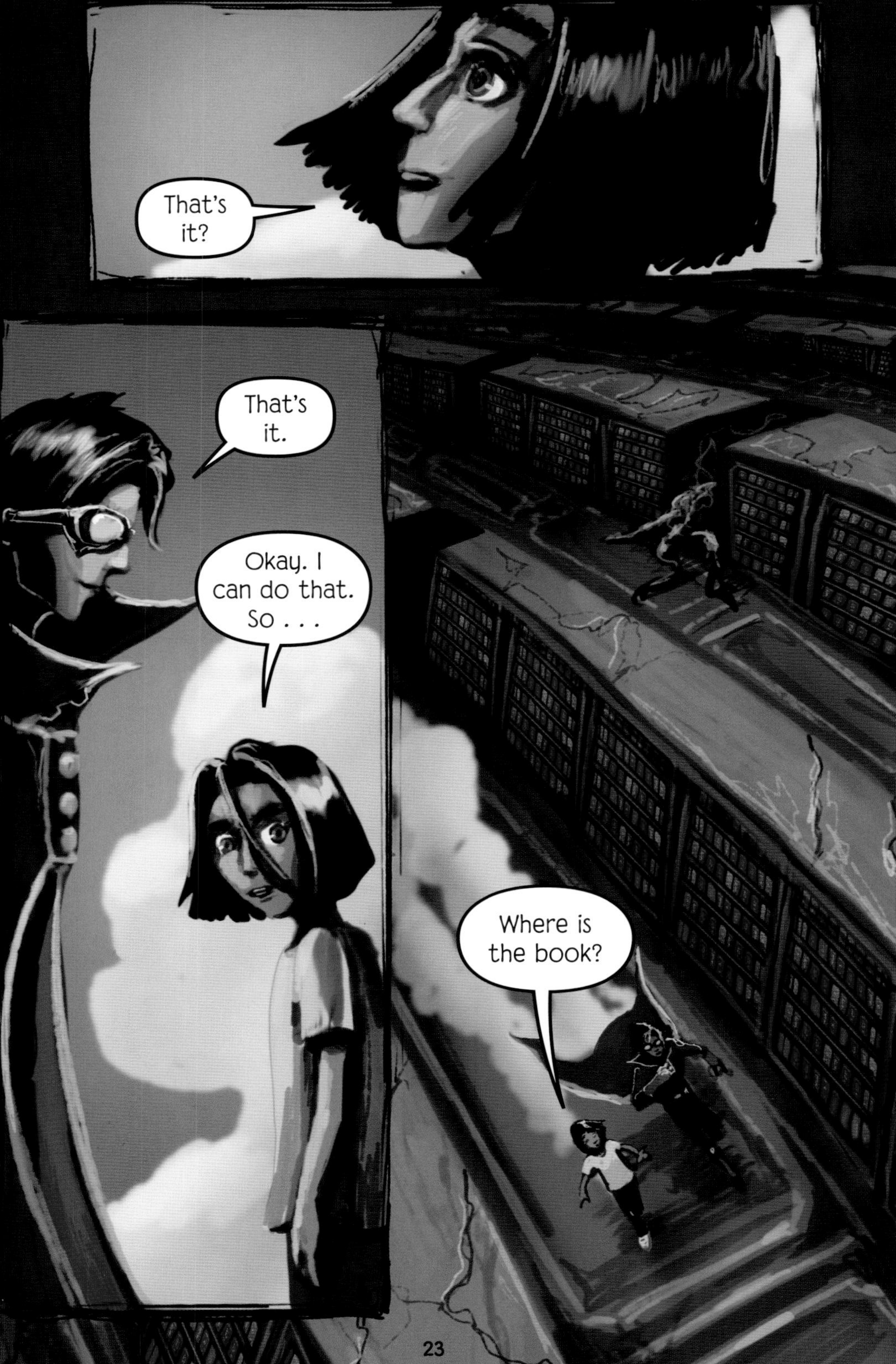
That's it?
That's it.
Okay. I can do that. So . . .
Where is the book?

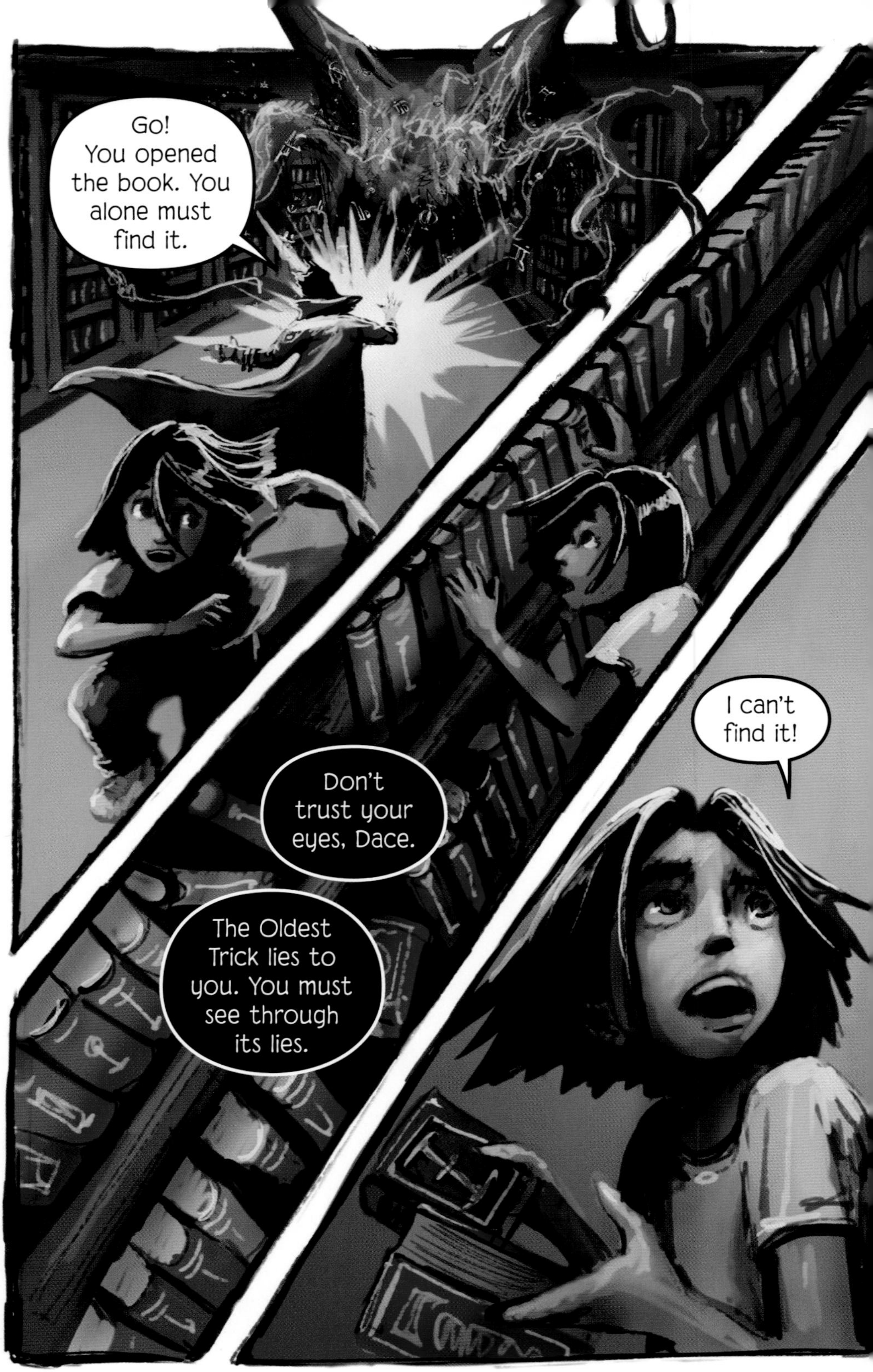
Go! You opened the book. You alone must find it.
Don't trust your eyes, Dace.
The Oldest Trick lies to you. You must see through its lies.
I can't find it!

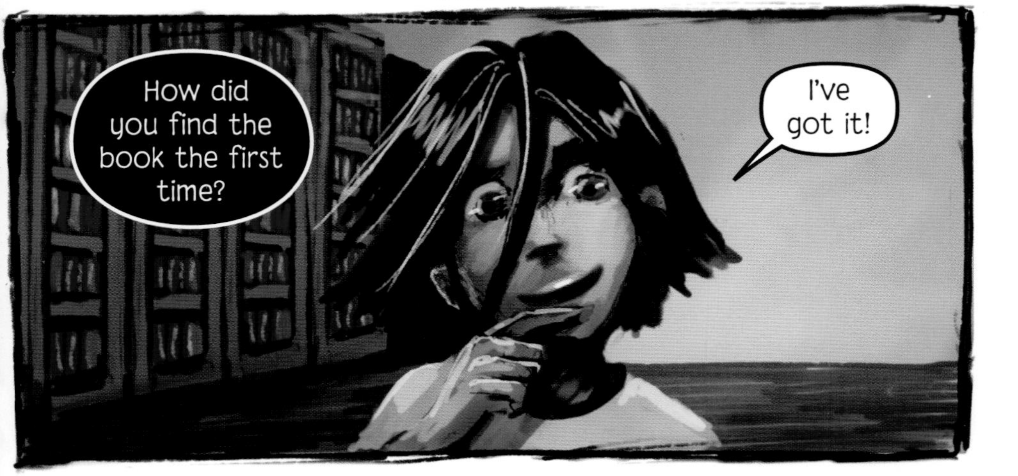
How did you find the book the first time?
I've got it!

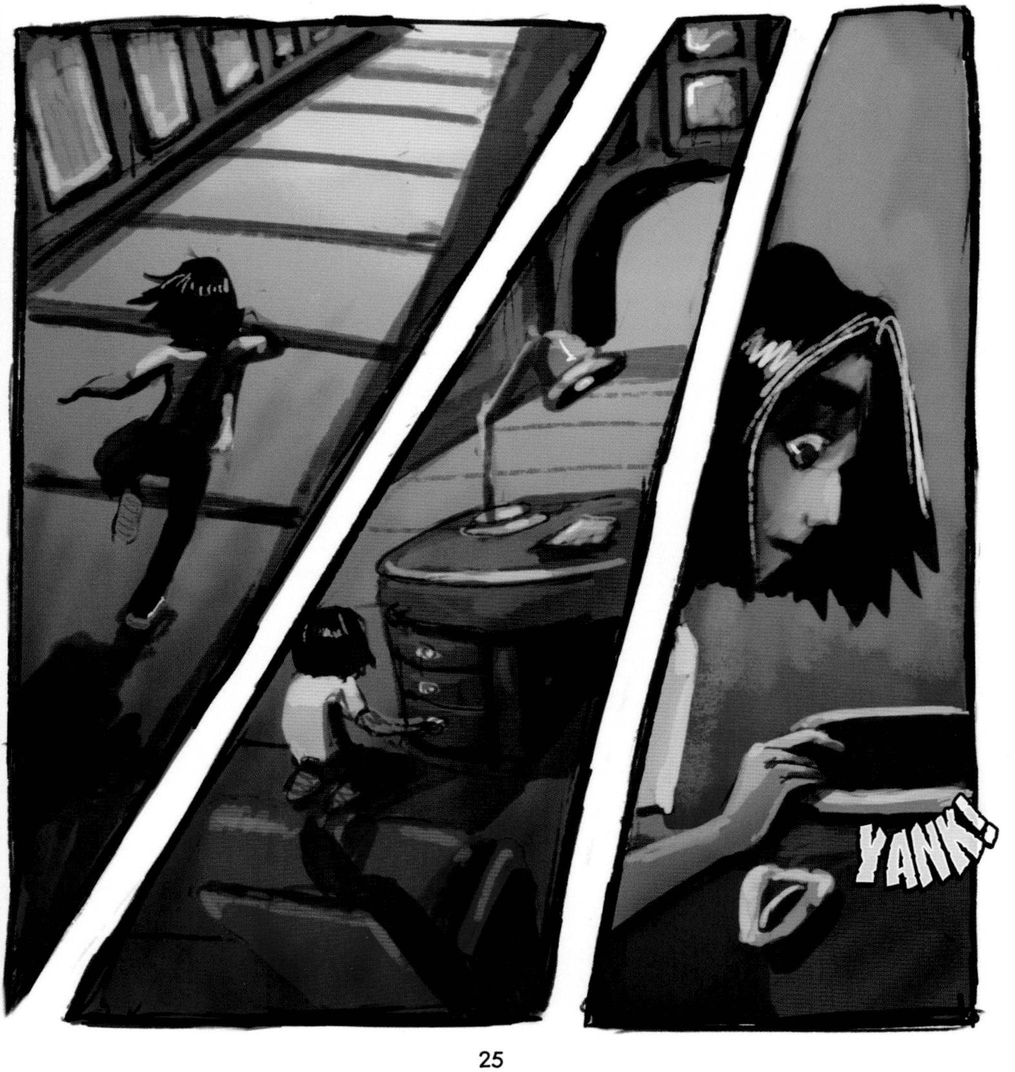
YANK!

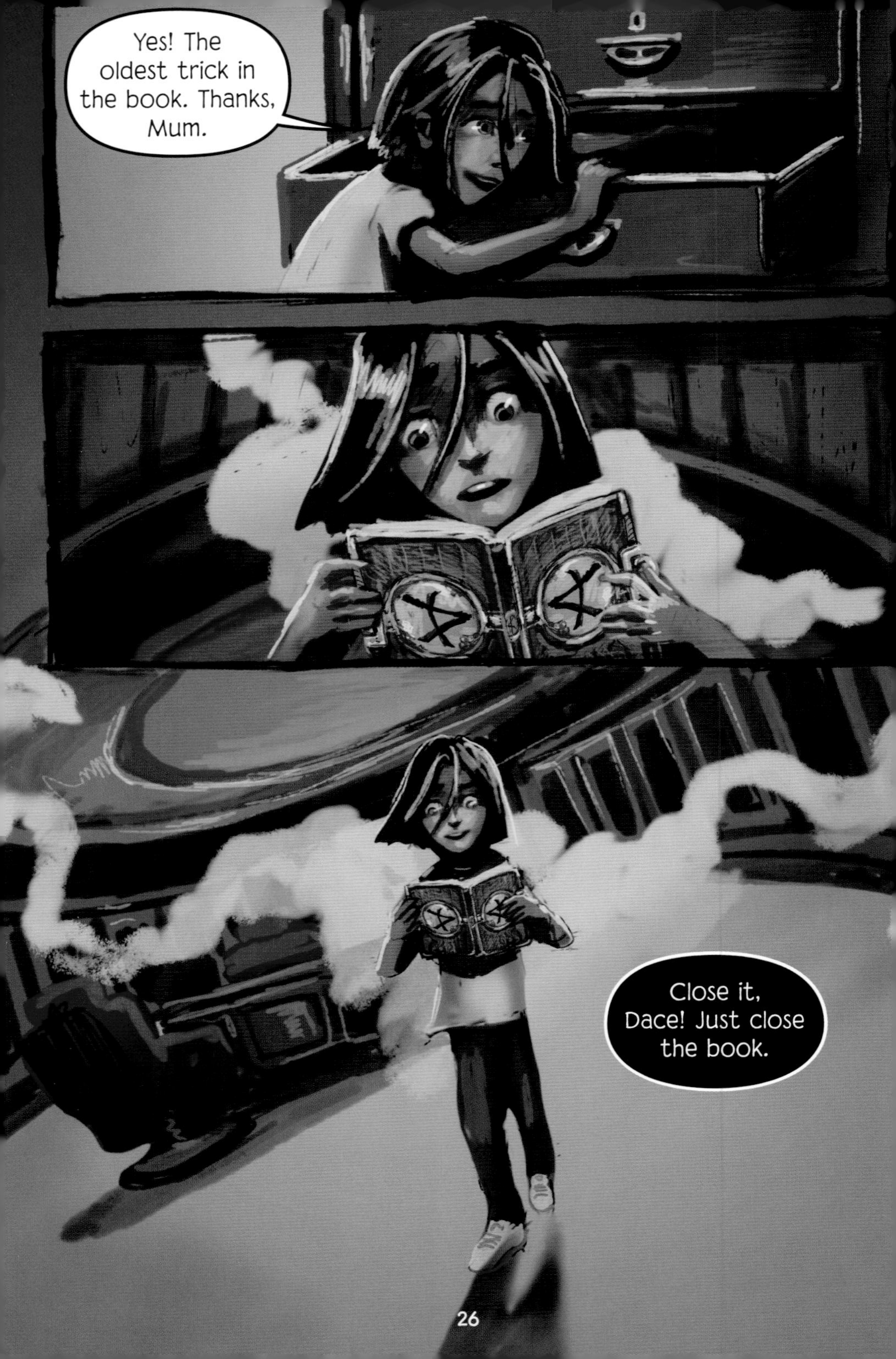
Yes! The oldest trick in the book. Thanks, Mum.
Close it, Dace! Just close the book.

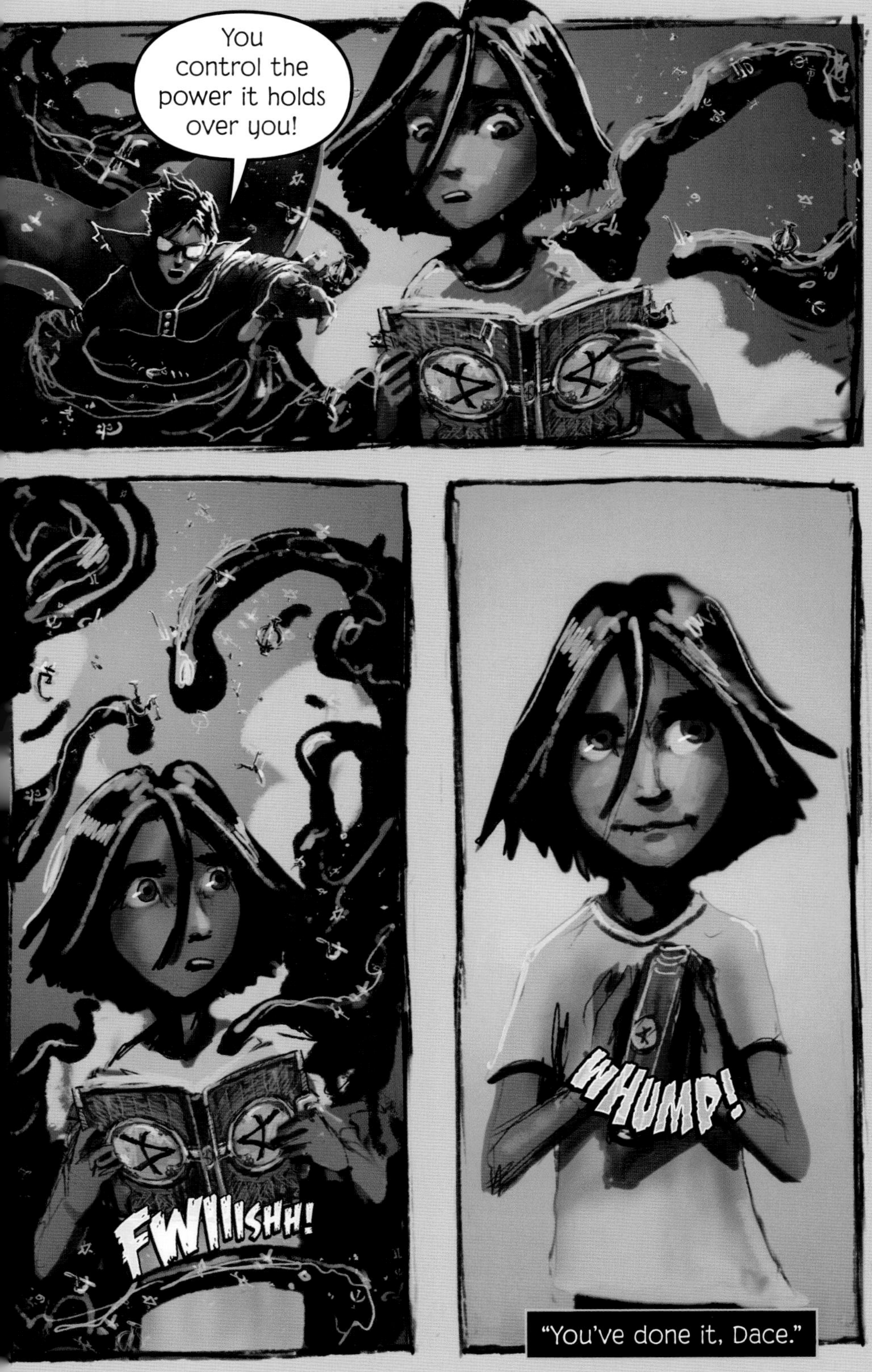
You control the power it holds over you!
FWIIISHH!
WHUMP!
"You've done it, Dace."

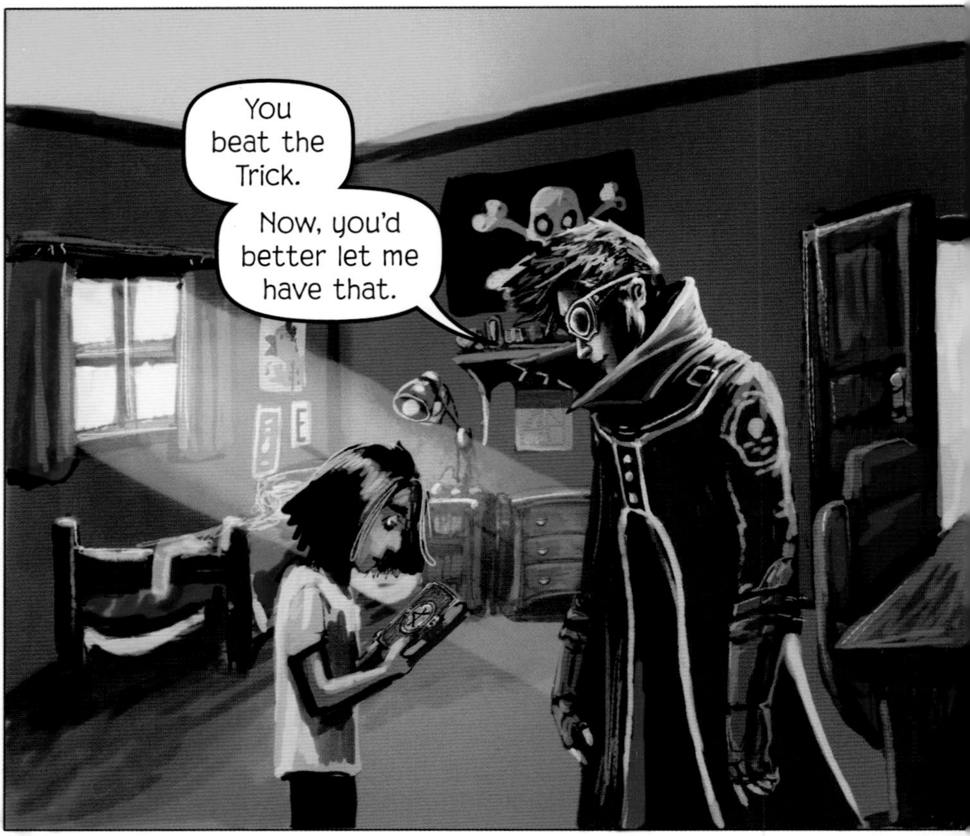
You beat the Trick.
Now, you'd better let me have that.

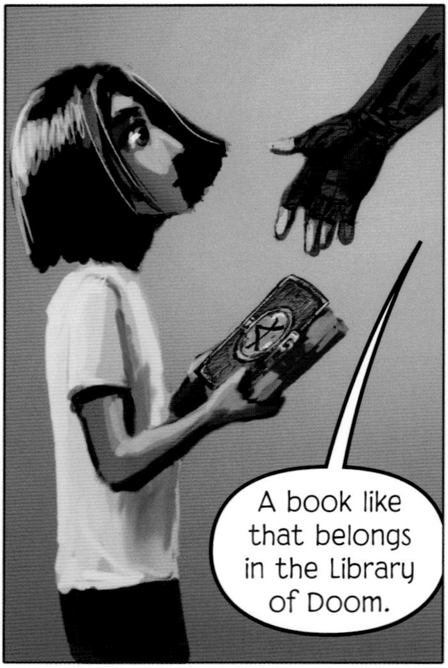
A book like that belongs in the Library of Doom.

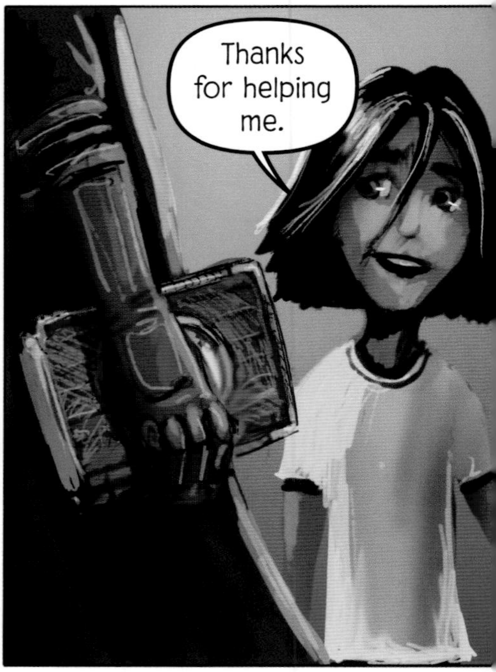
Thanks for helping me.

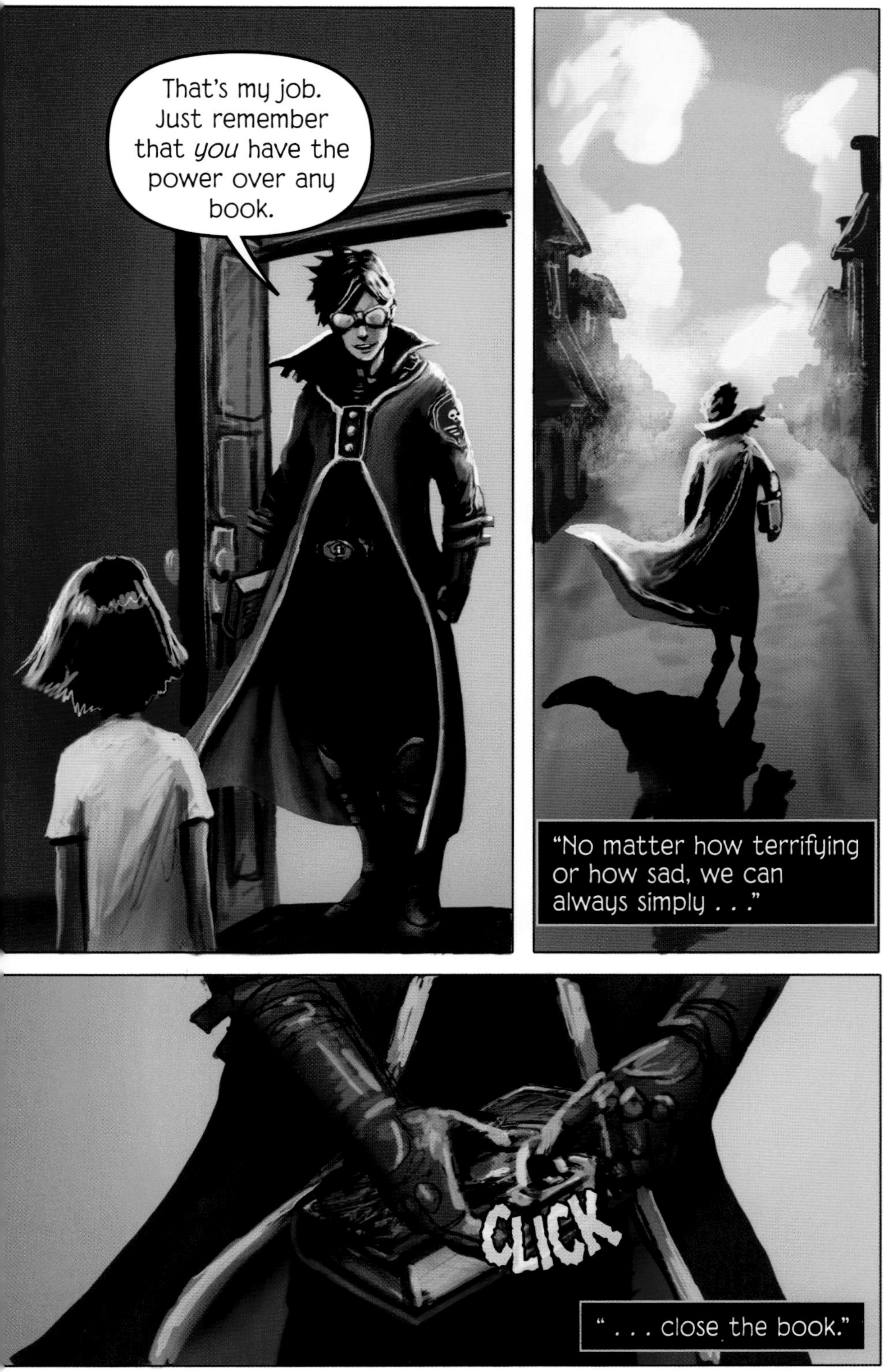
That's my job. Just remember that *you* have the power over any book.
"No matter how terrifying or how sad, we can always simply . . ."
CLICK
" . . . close the book."

LOOK CLOSER

1

The *Oldest Trick* traps Dace's mind. Look back in the story and find at least three clues in the art that show he's in the nightmare world.

2

Would you have tried to open the ancient book? Explain your answer.

3

No matter. In my shop, items tend to find who *they* are looking for.

Describe the shop owner in your own words. Do you trust him? Why or why not?

GLOSSARY

ancient very old and from a long time ago

antique object, such as a piece of furniture or jewellery, that was made a long time ago

cast-off thing that has been thrown away or got rid of

curiosities unusual, and sometimes rare, objects

knick-knack small object that is meant mostly for decoration

startle surprise or scare someone suddenly, often without meaning to

symbol mark or drawing that stands for something and has a specific meaning

terrifying causing a great deal of fear

torment cause pain and stress to the mind or body over a long period of time

ABOUT THE WRITER

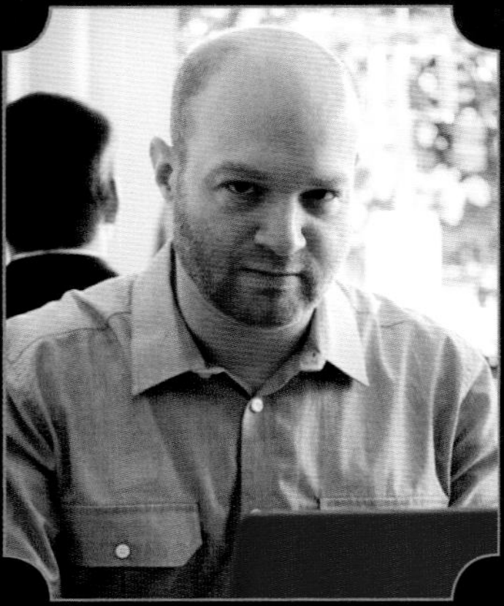

STEVE BREZENOFF is the author of more than fifty children's chapter books, including the series Field Trip Mysteries, Ravens Pass and Return to Titanic. He has also written three young adult novels, *Guy in Real Life*; *Brooklyn, Burning*; and *The Absolute Value of -1*. In his spare time, he enjoys video games, cycling and cooking. Steve lives in Minnesota, USA, with his wife, Beth, and their son and daughter.

ABOUT THE ARTIST

PATRICIO CLAREY was born in Argentina. He graduated in fine arts from the Martín A. Malharro School of Visual Arts, specializing in illustration and graphic design. Patricio currently lives in Barcelona, Spain, where he works as a freelance graphic designer and illustrator. He has created several comics and graphic novels, and his work has been featured in books and other publications.

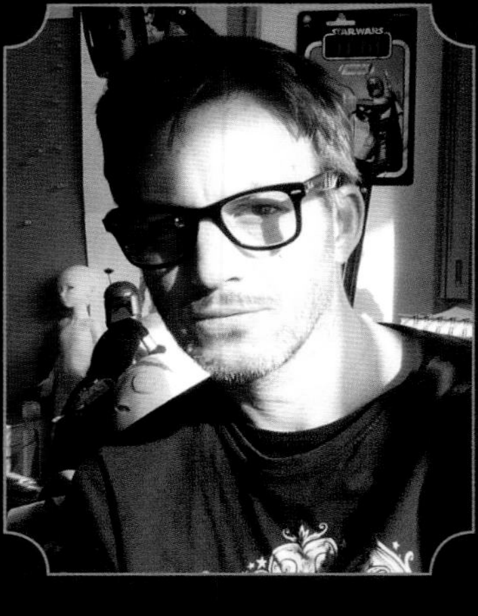
STAR WARS